# THE <u>ADVENTURES</u> OF GLIBB REDUNDANT PEOPLE, CRITTERS, AND NEW FRIENDS

*Ken Blanton*

Copyright © 2023 **Blanton Books Publishing**

All rights reserved. No part of this publication may be reproduced, distributed, or transmitted in any form or by any means, including photocopying, recording, or other electronic or mechanical methods, without the prior written permission of the publisher, except in the case of brief quotations embodied in critical reviews and certain other noncommercial uses permitted by copyright law. For permission requests, write to the publisher, addressed "Attention: Book Rights and Permission," at the address below.

Published in the United States of America

ISBN 978-1-960684-60-8 (SC)
ISBN 978-1-960684-59-2 (Ebook)

**Blanton Books Publishing**
Bowling Green, Kentucky 42101
http://blantonbookspublishing.com/

Ordering Information and Rights Permission:

Quantity sales. Special discounts might be available on quantity purchases by corporations, associations, and others. For details, contact the publisher at the address above.

For Book Rights Adaptation and other Rights Permission. Call us at toll-free 1-888-945-8513 or send us an email at admin@stellarliterary.com.

Glibb Redundant had a wonderful summer vacation from school. He enjoyed living on the family farm in the Midwest, especially in the summer. He loved fishing in his family's pond and watching all the crops grow. His dad was preparing to harvest the fields of crops soon. The new school year started today and due to visiting relatives, the evening before, Glibb was so tired this morning that he was not his normally excited self. His aunt, uncle and cousins had stayed well beyond his normal bedtime last evening. Glibb found himself wishing that he could have a couple more hours of sleep before getting up this morning. He found the strength to crawl out of his bed and get ready for the first day of school in the fourth grade. He yawned and stretched all the way to the bathroom.

Glibb returned to his room to get dressed after taking a shower and brushing his teeth. He made his bed and was on his way down stairs to breakfast. He was so glad that he could ride his bike, as he felt too tired to walk all the way to school this morning. He had dressed himself in a pair of new pants and shirt his mom had purchased him for the new school year. He left his lucky hat on the bedpost. He did not normally wear his lucky hat to school. He decided not to wear the new hat his mom surprised him with, as the bill of the cap needed to be bent to keep the sun from his eyes. He did not feel like trying to do any hat fixing this morning.

Glibb ate his breakfast and got ready to leave for school. He said goodbye to his mom and went outside to his bike. He mounted his bike and was off to school. The fresh morning air in his face seemed to help him feel more awake and served to stop him from yawning. His new bike seemed harder than normal to pedal.

The distance to school seemed much longer to him this day. He placed his bike in the bike rack and went into the school. The busses were arriving as he stopped at the bike rack. He entered the front door and walked briskly down the hallway to the bulletin board, so that he could read it before all the children came through the doors. He read the teachers and room numbers assigned list for the fourth grade, so he could realize his classroom number and teacher for this year. He recalled that his teacher's name was Mrs. Jones, but did not know the room number. Mrs. Jones was helping a few children find their assigned classrooms. They were collected around her desk, when

Glibb entered the classroom. They had not referenced the bulletin board. They had apparently arrived early too.

Glibb went back out of the classroom to go to the restroom while the teacher was busy. When Glibb returned to his classroom, the teacher was taking roll. She called his name as he came through the door in the middle of a yawn. He could not answer Mrs. Jones, so he raised his arm and waived it about in the air. All the seated children in the classroom roared with laughter at him walking into the room yawning and waiving his arm about, instead of answering the teacher.

The teacher did not find any humor with Glibb's actions, causing a disturbance in her classroom. Mrs. Jones stood up from her desk and pointed at a desk in the front row and directed Gibb to sit there, so she could keep an eye on him. He had been in school a very short time and had already made his teacher upset with him.

Glibb made it through the first day in the fourth grade without creating himself any more problems with the teacher. He had a very hard time staying awake and yawned often, but put his hand up to cover the yawn each time. The teacher gave each student an assignment to be turned in for grading in two weeks. Glibb thought that his assignment would take a few trips to the public library if he wanted to get an excellent grade. He realized that the two weeks would pass quickly. He might get busy with other things in the mean time and not have it completed on time. He decided to complete the assignment as soon as possible so that he would be ready to turn in on time. Glibb was so glad when the school bell rang to announce the first day of school was over.

Glibb walked down the hallway with a few of his classmates, which were also riding their bikes to school. They were discussing playing football for a while in a nearby park. Glibb informed them that he was going to the public library to start on his assignment so he could get it finished. Then he could play football without worrying about not having his report completed. His classmates teased him a little and then turned their efforts to choosing sides for the football game in the park.

Glibb yawned a few times while walking down the hallway with his classmates and again at the bike rack. Once he was outside for a minute, he seemed to become wide-awake. He folded his paper with his assignment listed, and stuffed it into his back pocket. He placed his books he was given for the new school year on the seat of his bike and placed the book strap tightly around them. He then strapped the books onto his bike's back luggage rack with a stretchy strap and mounted his bike to go to the public library located a block away. He waived to his classmates as he rode off toward the library. He arrived in a short time at the library and parked his bike in the bike rack.

The weather was excellent for bike riding and the wind and sunlight seemed to serve to perk Glibb up a bit. He had stopped yawing. The other boys did not want to go to the library today, but they might have to spend their weekend trying to get the assignment completed. Glibb would hopefully be finished with his.

Once inside the library, Glibb looked inside the index cabinet for the row and shelf where his subject's reference books would be found. The teacher had a few books listed for him on the piece of paper that he had previously folded and placed into his back pocket. He carefully pulled the folded paper from his back pocket. He had a hard time straightening the wrinkles and creases so he could write on the paper. He wrote the row and shelf on his sheet and replaced the card into the index and closed the drawer. He had his pencil placed behind his ear and it came in handy to write down the information from the index card.

The top of the sheet of paper had the assignment listed." The American War of independence" was the subject he was assigned. Glibb found the row and then noticed a paper sign listing "Early American History". He took several books down one at a time. Each one was all text with no pictures included in each book. He spotted a large book on the shelf with a title that read," The American War of Independence – Fully illustrated ". Glibb thought that this was the book for him to use. He carefully pulled the book from the shelf, as it was heavy. There was a table and chairs near by and Glibb took the book to the table and sat down in the nearest chair. He opened the book and was amazed at the full color pictures inside.

The first picture was of people dressed funny with long hair and three-cornered hats. The people in the picture had guns and were probably soldiers, but their uniforms looked very different than military uniforms he had ever seen.

Glibb was excited with the book and was glad that he had found it on the shelf. He began to read some of the text as he turned through the pages and looked at the pictures. The first part of the book was about the King of England and the American Colonies. He thumbed through the book, mainly looking at the pictures.

Glibb stopped at a picture of a white horse with a big guy mounted on its back yielding a sword. Other men were around him, with some being in uniforms. All the men around the guy on the horse had strange looking guns. A few pages deeper into the book, the guy on the horse was then in a boat. He was standing up with his long sword pointed ahead as the men with him in the boat were rowing. There were so many men in the boat that there was not much space for the men to move the oars. The boat was in a river with big trees covering the banks on each side.

Glibb decided to read about the picture with the men in the boat. He wanted to learn what the picture was about. He was curious about learning about the guy with the white horse. He was on the boat in the picture he was currently viewing with his sword drawn.

He seemed to be leading everyone. He read about the guy and realized it was a guy named George Washington. He read about very cold weather in the winter during the war between the King of England and the Continental army. Some of the soldiers had no shoes to wear. He read more about George

Washington. The picture was about George Washington and his soldiers crossing the Delaware River in a boat. Glibb was feeling sleepy but wanted to be sure this was the book he would check out and use for his report. He continued to read.

All of a sudden Glibb found himself standing in a clearing on the riverbank. Poorly dressed soldiers were all around. Some soldiers were dragging a boat to the riverbank. They stopped at the bank as if they were waiting for some reason. A big white horse with a big guy mounted in the saddle was riding into the clearing. It was George Washington on the horse. The big white horse stopped close to the place where Glibb was standing. George Washington dismounted the horse, as a soldier came to meet the horse, taking the reins. The soldier addressed the guy that was on the horse as General Washington and led his horse off and tied the reins to a small tree. Several men followed the General to the boat with their rifles in hand.

Glibb climbed into the boat with the soldiers and General Washington. The General was standing in the front of the boat with his sword drawn and pointed ahead as the boat was floating toward the middle of the river. Glibb was standing in the boat very close to a soldier manning an oar. The soldiers were trying to get the boat across the river fast and the oars were moving back and forth quickly. Glibb got too close to the soldier manning an oar and fell over the side when bumped. The water was ice cold on his head.

His head came above the water to hear a thundering of hundreds of guns firing almost at the same time.

Glibb suddenly realized that he was back at the library, sitting in the chair at the table with his head on the tabletop. The gun noise he was hearing was actually his snoring. He had fallen asleep. He realized his head was wet. "How could this be," he wondered. He felt for the book as he opened his eyes. He then raised his head a little to view the librarian, Mrs. Brown standing on the other side of the table with an empty water glass in her right hand and the book he was reading in the other. "I tried to wake you with a shake, but you snored louder, so I poured my glass of water on your head," She explained. "This is a library and I had to stop the noise you were making. You disturbed the others in the library that are trying to read," She continued. Glibb felt the ice-cold water running down his back and neck as he set straight up in the chair. "Can I check this book out and take it home with me?" Glibb asked Mrs. Brown. "You can check it out if you have a library card. Then it might remain quiet in the library," She responded.

She placed the book on the end of the table away from the water as she wiped the water from the table where Glibb was setting. "Get some sleep before coming here and causing problems for the people trying to read," Mrs. Brown stated to Glibb, as she went to throw the paper towel away. "Yes Mrs. Brown," Glibb responded. He got up from sitting at the table, picked up the book from the end of the table, went to the counter and checked out the book. He exited the front door of the library. He strapped the book onto his bike's luggage rack on top of the other books, as it was too big and heavy for his book strap, or for him to carry while riding his bike.

Glibb mounted his bike and took a deep breath. He realized how real it all seemed although he was only dreaming. He had learned a lot today. He thought that he could surely get a very good grade for his assignment report.

Glibb was on his way home. The wind made him shiver at first due to his wet neck and head. Glibb thought that if he had worn his lucky hat today, his head would probably still be dry. He was glad he found such an interesting book to read for his assignment. He felt wide-awake as he rode his bike home.

Glibb shared the library book with his mom and dad after supper. He told them about falling asleep in the library and being awaken by Mrs. Brown, the librarian, when she poured ice-cold water on his head. He told his parents the complete story about his snoring loudly and not waking when she shook him. They had a laugh and ensured Glibb that he would be getting in bed early this night and always through the week, now that school is in session. Glibb nodded in agreement.

Glibb would leave the book at home and read it after school every day. He looked at the pictures several times after he finished reading the book. The people amazed him being dressed so differently. There were few houses in the pictures. The houses pictured were fine white houses and occasionally small houses that looked like shacks. Glibb had his assignment completed a week early.

Glibb could now play ball with his friends after school if he wanted.

Glibb took the amazing book back to the library to return it earlier than the librarian expected. Mrs. Brown was very nice to him since he was not disrupting the library. Glibb decided that Mrs. Brown was actually a very nice lady.

It was the morning of the day Glibb was to read his assignment paper to the class. He had a good night's sleep and was anxious to read his report to all his classmates. Glibb was ready for school and had finished his breakfast earlier than usual this day. He said goodbye to his mom, retrieved his books and went outside to his bike. He was leaving a little early for school, to have time to rehearse reading the report. He read his report to his parents last night and they seemed to enjoy hearing it. They told him that he did a fine job researching for his assignment. He neatly folded his report and slid it into the back pocket of his new jeans and was off to school.

Glibb was pedaling his bike to make it go pretty fast so he could get to school in plenty of time to rehearse. He was looking around and not paying much attention to the path he was taking. A black and white animal wondered into his path. Glibb noticed it in his path too late to swerve and miss the critter. Glibb's new bike's front wheel hit the critter, running right over it. This threw Glibb off the bike onto the ground. The critter was all shook up and ran around in ever widening circles. The critter was heading toward Glibb as he was sitting up to assess the damage to his elbow. The critter came up to Glibb and turned his backside to him, lifted its tail and thoroughly sprayed Glibb's front side. The critter then wandered toward the forest nearby and disappeared in the tall grass. Glibb raised his arms to protect his face from the spray at the last moment. Glibb, realized that he had hit and disoriented a big skunk. He instinctively knew what to expect when it raised its tail toward him.

Glibb's hands protected his face and eyes. He could hardly breath due to the strong stench. The skunk spray stunk terribly. A skunk had never sprayed him before. Glibb wrongly thought that the wind would dry the spray and the smell would go away. He decided that his elbow was scraped a little but was all right. He checked his scratched new bike for the extent of damages. There were only a few scratches, so he got back on the bike and continued on his way to school. His clothes were covered with the foul smelling spray. These were brand new school clothes, Glibb thought. He was hopeful that the stink could be washed away when his mom did the laundry.

Glibb decided to continue on to school instead of going home to change clothes and wash off the stinking skunk spray. Glibb arrived at school before any of the other children. He placed his bike in the bike rack and retrieved his books from the rear luggage rack and headed toward the front door of the school. He arrived at the door and saw nobody in the hallway. He opened the door and started down the hall. The school secretary was at her desk reviewing a stack of papers and did not notice Glibb passing by. As soon as he walked by her desk, her eyes and nose were greatly affected. Her eyes started tearing and her nose smelled a very pungent odor. The stench was familiar to her, but it was so strong. She began to sneeze. She grabbed her nose with her hand to close her nostrils and yelled, "P U, it stinks in here." By this time Glibb was down at the boys rest room. He had decided that washing his hands would possibly help to eliminate the odor that remained and to wash his dirty arms. He could not smell the stench very much himself.

His nose was quite used to the odor. The School secretary called the janitor as soon as she stopped sneezing for a moment. She urgently stated to him "A skunk has entered the building and I can't stand this stench." The janitor promised that he would be there to correct the matter in a few moments. Glibb overheard part of the call before entering the restroom. He thought she had a problem that did not concern him. He proceeded to wash his hands. The soap dispenser was out of soap. He wetted his hands and arms in the sink and then wiped them on the cotton towel that was hanging from the towel machine.

Glibb picked up his books and left the rest room. Glibb noticed the janitor with a mask on his face, as he entered the hallway again. The janitor was mopping the floor at the front door entry area of the school. He did not realize that it was because of him. He noticed the secretary was standing outside of the front door holding her nose. He walked down the hall toward his classroom. He found the door at the front of the classroom locked. He knew the door at the other end was probably unlocked, so he tried that door. He found that door unlocked so he opened it and walked inside. He walked briskly to his assigned desk and placed his books on his desk. He reached behind himself to retrieve his report from his back pocket. He carefully unfolded the pages and straightened the creases. He started rehearsing his reading of the report out loud. He was glad the water had washed the dirt from his hands and arms. He did not want to soil his assignment papers.

Meanwhile the busses were arriving with the children. The janitor had neutralized the skunk stench from the front door and the disinfectant was overwhelmingly strong at the front door. The janitor opened the door for the secretary to enter. She went to the principle's office and shut the door. The strong odors could not be smelled as much in there. She carried her work with her to try to complete it. The children bolted through the front door as they always do. The first few children stopped in their tracks and held their noses because the cleanser was so strong. The fumes made them sick and all the children ran to the rest rooms. The boys all yelled "PU" after entering the boy's rest room. Glibb had transferred the strong stench of the skunk to the sink and towel in the room. All the boys ran out into the hall and out the front door. They were giving up their breakfasts when the janitor asked them what was the problem. They told the janitor that the boy's rest room smelled like a skunk. The janitor put the mask back on and went to the boy's rest room to clean it.

More children were arriving to school. They asked the classmates outside what was going on. They all decided to stay outside until all the school was safe to enter. The secretary had completed her paper work and went outside to instruct the children to go to their classrooms.

The children went back into the hallway and quickly to their rooms. Glibb's classmates entered the classroom through the back door and most were inside before they smelled the stench Glibb was wearing. They all grabbed their nose, gagged and exited the room yelling "PU" as they ran down the hallway.

It was time for Mrs. Jones to arrive for class and take roll. She wondered why the children were running down the hallway the wrong way. She unlocked the main door to the classroom. She opened the door and entered. The stench hit her within two steps into the room. She ran to the windows and opened one. She stuck her head out of the window for a couple minutes. She turned to Glibb and asked him what was stinking so badly. Glibb explained that he had hit a skunk with his bike and got sprayed this morning on the way to school. Glibb told her that he thought the wind would make the stink go away. She opened a couple more windows and called the janitor on her cell phone. The janitor came in with his respirator mask and helped the teacher open all the windows. The janitor told Glibb to crawl through the window and go home to get cleaned and free of the skunk stench.

Glibb carefully folded his papers and placed them back into his back pocket. He then walked over to the windows and crawled through a window opening to drop onto the lawn outside. Mrs. Jones called Glibb's mom to inform her of his condition and that he is headed home. The janitor then had the teacher call a commercial company to neutralize the stench throughout the building. The principle arrived to school at this point and cancelled school for the day.

Glibb arrived at his bike and everyone standing around the front of the school building held their nose, parted and scattered to get away from him and the stench. He mounted his bike and started toward his family farm. He had left his books in the classroom, but the books would be there tomorrow. Glibb laughed at the funny sight of all the children running while holding their nose.

Glibb's mom was sitting on the front porch swing waiting for him to arrive. She had placed a big round tub in the yard, half full of tomato juice. His mom did not want him to stink up the house. Glibb noticed the tub as he turned into the driveway. He recalled his dad and uncle discussing tomato juice as a good thing to get the skunk smell from a hunting dog. He was wondering if it would do the same for him. It took over an hour for the tomato juice bath to make the skunk stench go away. Glibb could almost smell things again. His mom had to help him get out of the big tub. He was rinsed with a garden hose until the juice was mostly gone from him. His mom used a long stick to pick up his clothes from the ground. She placed them in a fire barrel, to burn. She had started a fire in the barrel while Glibb was taking the tomato juice bath. Glibb dried himself with towels on the front porch and got dressed into his clean play clothes. His mom came over and sniffed him all over to ensure the stench was totally gone. Glibb passed his mom's inspection. He then went to his bike and poured tomato juice over it since it stunk as he did earlier. He washed it off with the garden hose and repeated the bike's bath several times. Half of the tomato juice had been used to make his bike not stink. There were signs of tomato juice all over the yard. He carefully wiped the bike dry as he sniffed to ensure that the entire stench was gone from his bike.

Glibb was glad that he had copied his report to make it look neat, since his mom burned the report that he had folded in his pants back pocket. He could turn in the one that is a little messy rather than have to write the report again. Glibb's mom called the teacher Mrs. Jones to let her know that he no longer smelled as a skunk. Mrs. Jones informed Glibb's mom that the school was much better after commercial treatment and school will be in session tomorrow.

Glibb was up early and ready for school with his bed made before his mom had breakfast cooked the next morning. He ate breakfast and was ready to leave for school early with his report in his back pocket. Glibb's dad came in from the fields late yesterday and did not say much to Glibb about the chaos he had caused at school. This morning during breakfast, his dad just sniffed at him and stated his approval, that all seemed back to normal. Glibb had a great night's sleep. He rode his bike to school quickly this morning, arriving early at the school. The janitor was standing outside the front door. Glibb placed his bike in the bike rack and walked toward the front door. The janitor stopped him and carefully sniffed him, before allowing him to enter the building. The school smelled inside like a hospital. Glibb though that he had never known the school to be this clean before. He found the same classroom door locked, but the other was open. When he entered the room it was clean and smelled fresh. He sat at his desk and again reviewed his report. All his books had been wiped and smelled fresh. His book strap was wrapped around them and did not stink as before. Mrs. Jones called on Glibb to give his report first, after she took roll.

Everyone applauded him after he read his report. Mrs. Jones was impressed with his report and his presentation. Mrs. Jones informed him that he would receive an "A" grade for his assignment. She sniffed him and commented that he had a much more acceptable fragrance that yesterday. He thanked her and sat down at his desk. She could hardly believe that the entire stench was gone. His new friend Joe was in his class but was not present today to hear him read his report. Glibb was hopeful that he had not made Joe sick with the stench yesterday.

The bell rang and this school day was finally over. Glibb rarely saw Joe's brother John in school as he was in the fifth grade. He wondered if John was at school today. He could have made him sick too. Glibb thought that he would see them both tomorrow. Glibb was anxious to get home and show his mom the grade he received for his assignment. He had put a lot of effort into the report and the "A" grade made it all worthwhile.

Glibb was on the way home on his bike. He was crossing a short bridge over a creek as he did every day to and from school. He noticed a couple of kids his age poking at things in the creek with sticks. They were not far from the road, walking in the creek bed. He recognized the boys. They were Joe and John. What were they doing in the creek bed, instead of attending school today, Glibb wondered. Glibb enjoyed school and never missed school unless he was ill. Glibb shouted to the brothers as he stopped his bike on the bridge. They were busy poking at things with sticks and did not notice Glibb. The brothers started to run back towards the woods, but Joe recognized Glibb. They climbed the creek bank onto the shoulder of the road and onto the bridge where Glibb was sitting on his bike.

"Why were you guys not in school today?" Glibb asked. John said" We figured that it would take a few days to get the stink out of the school. We did not ask if there was school today, we just decided to play hooky," John continued. Joe nodded in agreement. Glibb coasted beside the brothers as they walked toward their home. "I never thought of playing hooky from school because I like learning stuff," Glibb shared. John responded, "We think that school is a waste of time." Joe nodded in agreement. They came to the driveway to Glibb's parent's farm. They all said goodbye and Glibb rode up the driveway and parked his bike in the yard. The brothers continued on to their house.

Glibb told his mom about getting an "A" on his assignment. When his dad came in from his work on the farm, Glibb's mom told him the good news about their son's excellent grade. His parents were very proud of their son. He was doing well in school in spite of his confrontation with a skunk. Glibb seemed to have focus and direction with his schoolwork.

Glibb was out of bed early this day, as it was Friday and the last day of the second week of the new school year. School could get weary after a couple weeks of learning new things until a person got used to it, Glibb thought. He made his bed and got ready for school. After breakfast he said goodbye to his mom, collected his books and went outside to his bike for the ride to school. Once outside he realized it was a foggy morning.

Glibb thought he saw people walking up the road in the fog. He rode his bike to the end of the driveway. Just before turning toward the direction of the school, he heard someone call his name. It sounded familiar to him. It was John and Joe. Glibb turned his bike toward the voice he heard. John and Joe appeared from the thick fog. Glibb asked, "Are you guys planning on going to school today, or playing hooky?" John replied, "We plan to play hooky, are you in for some fun today?" Glibb said," I don't know for sure." "Hold up a minute and we will talk about it," John replied. John and Joe made playing hooky sound like a lot of fun, as they tried to convince Glibb to join them instead of going on to school.

Glibb decided that there was some time before school so he would see what playing hooky was all about. They walked beside Glibb as they progressed on the roadside to the bridge over the creek. John instructed Glibb to put his bike in the ditch and come with them. They waited for Glibb to put his bike in the ditch and then all the boys repelled down the creek bank to the creek bed. The brothers had cigarettes and they lit one each. They offered one to Glibb, but he shook his head to inform them that his answer was no. They did not try to convince him as they recalled what had happened at the barn after the fish fry. They had gone fishing that day and had a fish fry. Glibb tried to light a cigarette, turned all different colors in his face and got sick all over Joes shoes. That resulted in getting the brothers in trouble.

The brothers smoked their cigarettes as Glibb looked on. He looked around for a place to sit. The creek was low and had very little flowing water. There was not much to do but poke at things with sticks, Glibb thought. Glibb asked the brothers, "What are you going to do all day, besides smoke cigarettes?" John in response said, "look for stuff and find a good stick for poking at things in the creek."

"That is what I thought." Glibb said. "I enjoy school and learning new things. I grew up in the country and I have better things to do than poke at things with sticks." Glibb stated. John said, "Go to your dumb school then, but we will stay here and smoke and have fun."

"Fun is fishing or going to school and getting good grades and Sunday school class," Glibb stated. He then turned to start up the bank to go back to his bike and go to school. Joe yelled at Glibb asking him if he could get a ride to school with him. "It is too late to walk to school and get there on time," Joe explained. Glibb nodded a yes gesture and Joe climbed up the creek bank, to the bike following Glibb. John said nothing, as he was surprised at his younger brother's decision. Glibb got his bike onto the road and mounted, then Joe climbed on straddling the luggage rack mounted over the back fender. Joe held on to the back of Glibb's seat and they rode to school. As they were riding over the bridge of the creek, John yelled to them saying, "I will be having fun here while you guys are bored in that silly school all day!" Glibb told Joe to ignore his brother. "Your brother will be the only one to get in trouble and miss learning things in school today, not us," Glibb explained. Joe agreed that they were doing the smart thing by going to school.

Glibb was glad to finally get to school since he had to hold his books with his book strap in one hand while trying to keep control of his bike with Joe on the back. Glibb had never had someone ride on his bike with him before. Joe slid off the rear of the bike when they arrived at school. Glibb was glad, as it seemed so much lighter with only him on the bike. He placed the bike into the rack and caught up with Joe. They were barely arriving on time, but would not be tardy, or absent. Joe stated to Glibb his concern for his big brother, but that he did not want to get into trouble as his brother was to be soon.

The teacher asked Joe to come to her desk. He slowly walked to her desk, dragging his feet and trying to think of an excuse for missing school the day after the school was cleared of the skunk smell from Glibb. Mrs. Jones only wanted to know where his homework was. He sighed a sigh of relief and told her that he had left it at home and would be sure to bring it to her tomorrow, first thing. He then asked her what the homework assignment was. He was caught. Mrs. Jones informed him that she did not recall him being in class yesterday and that she had assigned no homework yesterday. She told Joe that he needed a note from his mom explaining why he had missed school that day. She told him to go to his desk and pay attention today. She knew that he and his brother had not been in school the day before and was glad to see him with Glibb. She knew how much Glibb liked attending school and learning new things. Mrs. Jones thought that Glibb might prove to be a positive influence for Joe. She thought that she would call Joe's mom and have a talk with her about Joe's absence yesterday. She would try to not make a big thing of it, as long as Joe missed no more days of school, unless he was ill.

Joe felt so stupid after he asked Mrs. Jones what the assignment was, after telling her he had done his homework and left it at home. He just knew that he would be in trouble and in the principle's office sometime that day. The bell rang to announce the end of the school day and Joe had not been in trouble yet. He thought that he was in the clear. Glibb picked up his books and placed them in his book strap. As he tightened the strap, Joe walked up to him and asked if he could ride with him to his driveway. Glibb told Joe that he could again ride on the back of his bike. They told their classmates they had to go and could not play ball this day. The bike was reclaimed from the bike rack and they both mounted. The bike was wobbling as Glibb first started pedaling with the added weight of Joe on the back. They both waived at their classmates as they rode off toward home.

They arrived at the bridge over the creek. Glibb stopped close to the side to see if John was in sight. John was down in the creek bed poking at things in the pools of water with a crooked stick. He had a cigarette in his hand between his fingers. Joe Yelled at him, "John, what are you poking at with your crooked stick?" John looked surprised and said, "Nothing that would be of interest to you" John asked how school was and if Joe learned anything. Joe said," I learned that I might get away with taking one day to playing hooky, but not two days in a row." John threw his stick down and climbed the bank to the bridge deck by Joe and Glibb. "Did you guys tell on me?' John asked in a rough voice. Glibb told John, "The teachers take attendance every morning. Do you think that they will not wonder where you were? The principle probably has called your mom already." Glibb continued. John said, "Oh well, it is not like I have not been in trouble before for missing school." Joe then stated, "John, school is not bad and they teach you stuff. Why miss out on learning and get in trouble too." Glibb nodded in agreement. "I will probably be in trouble for missing yesterday, but you will have to account for two days." "Let us go home to be punished, as I am finished with playing hooky and getting in trouble," Joe told his big brother. John looked at the ground and nodded his head, yes. They walked on toward their home beside Glibb on his bike, riding slowly beside the brothers until reaching his driveway. They said goodbye to Glibb as he rode up to his yard and parked his bike.

At dinner Glibb told his parents of the day's early morning fog. He informed them of all he learned in school during the day. His mom asked him where his friends John and Joe were. Glibb told them about the stopping at the creek this morning and deciding not to play hooky with John. Joe decided not to play hooky with his big brother, but rode to school with him on the back of his bike instead. Glibb's mom stated, "The boys' mom called to ask if I had noticed the boys around, as she had a call from the principle about the boys missing school this week. She informed me that Joe was at school today, but John was absent." Glibb's mom conveyed that she told her how glad she was that Glibb likes school and causes no problems. "Glibb should be a good example for your boys," Mrs. Redundant suggested. Mrs. Smith agreed and explained that her boys fell in with boys in the big city that frequently got into trouble. "We are so blessed to have moved to a small town," She conveyed to Mrs. Redundant. "Glibb and other children that attend Sunday school will prove to be good examples of acceptable behavior for my sons," She continued. They briefly discussed the differences between the big city and their small town. Glibb was so glad that he liked school and did not want to play hooky and miss learning things in school, especially since his friends were likely to be in trouble.

After dinner Glibb asked his dad if they were going fishing the next morning, as it will be Saturday. His dad said that he had accomplished a lot this week. "I can surely take one day off to go fishing with you son," His dad said. Glibb asked his dad if he could invite Joe and John to come fishing with him and his dad. His dad told him that it would be all right to invite his new friends. Glibb decided to call the brothers instead of riding his bike to their house, as it was almost dark.

The phone rang and Mrs. Smith answered the call. Glibb asked her if the brothers could go fishing with him and his dad tomorrow morning at 6:00. Mrs. Smith informed Glibb that both boys were being punished for playing hooky from school this week. "I know that Joe only missed one day of school, but he did play hooky from school and will be punished. John is receiving twice as much punishment for missing two days of school this week," Mrs. Smith explained. Glibb said, "Boy am I glad that I enjoy going to school." Mrs. Smith said, "If they behave and do as they should, the boys might be able to go fishing with you the next time you want them along." Glibb thanked Mrs. Smith for her time and explanation. After he placed the phone receiver down he shared what he had learned with his parents.

His dad had Glibb go to the front porch to sit with him a while before going to bed. His dad waited for both of them to become comfortable. He then said, "Glibb, I am concerned about you riding your bike to school on the main road, if you do not watch where you are going. A skunk is something that you would not want to hit with your bike. I understand that things happen. Just be extra aware of your surroundings and what is in your path. You could have landed in the road." He continued, "I am very proud of the excellent grade on your report. I am so relieved to realize that you did not follow others and play hooky this week. I am sure that the brothers would love to go fishing this weekend, with us. They decided to do wrong by playing hooky this week and are being punished. It is so much easier to do what is expected of you. That way parents are proud and all can have much more fun. I am so proud of you," His dad added. "Boy did you stink up the school the other day," His dad stated. "It will be great to fish with you this Saturday. Maybe we can catch a few big bass. By the way, you are not going to go swimming this time I hope," His dad, concluded. Glibb enjoyed most of this talk with his dad. He was so glad he had made the right decisions. He was so glad that he never thought very much about poking at things with sticks in creeks and ditches.

He did not tell his dad that he had convinced his friend Joe to come with him to school that morning, instead of playing hooky with his big brother. Glibb thought that it would sound like he was boasting. His dad does not appreciate people that brag or boast and he wanted his dad's approval.

The morning came too early on Saturday for Glibb to appreciate this day. He suddenly recalled that it was Saturday and he is to go fishing with his dad at the pond by 6"00 am. He bounced from his bed and quickly dressed. He put on his lucky hat and headed down to breakfast.

The end…

Printed by Libri Plureos GmbH in Hamburg, Germany